THE FORGETFUL BEARS HELP SANTA

by LARRY WEINBERG
illustrated by BRUCE DEGEN

Scholastic Inc.
New York   Toronto   London   Auckland   Sydney

To my wonderful Janie, who is unforgettable.
— L.W.

To Harry and Mildred
— B.D.

ISBN 0-590-40994-8

Text copyright © 1988 by Larry Weinberg.
Illustrations copyright © 1988 by Bruce Degen.
All rights reserved. Published by Scholastic Inc.

12 11 10 9 8 7 6 5 4 3 2 1   10   9/8 0 1 2 3 4/9

Printed in the U.S.A.

'Twas the night before Christmas, and all through the house . . . not a Forgetful remembered it was the night before Christmas.

Everyone was in bed and fast asleep when suddenly
there was a loud crash. Mrs. Forgetful opened her eyes.
She shook her husband. "Wake up!" she whispered. "I
think there's a burglar downstairs!"

"I'll take care of *that!*" exclaimed Mr. Forgetful,
rushing for the stairs.

But he forgot where they were and ran into the bathroom.

"Now what did I come here for?" he asked himself.
Then he saw in the mirror that his toothbrush was still
in his mouth. "Oh! To finish brushing, that's why! Now
if I could only remember which teeth I've done already."

Just then, he heard a voice that seemed to come from
the wall. "Ho ho ho! — and *help!* Someone forgot to fix
the chimney! And I'm stuck inside!"

"Brushing can wait!" cried Mr. Forgetful, running out
of the room.

He turned on the lights and found the stairs. "There
you are, you crook!" he cried as he ran down. "I've got
you now!"

"Will you please take your paws off me!" shouted
Grandpa Forgetful. "I am your father!"

"Oh. Are you really?"

"Yes! But I thought I heard you calling that you were
stuck in the chimney."

"Hmm. I wonder why I did that?" said Mr. Forgetful,
scratching his head. "Well, anyway, I'm all right now."

"But I'm not! Ho ho ho!" cried a voice from the
fireplace.

Looking up the chimney, Mr. Forgetful saw a man with a long white beard and a bright red suit. He wagged his finger at the man. "Shame on you! Sneaking into houses like that! If we let you go, will you promise not to do it again?"

"Oh, I wasn't sneaking! Well . . . yes, I was . . . ho ho ho! But for a good reason."

Mrs. Forgetful came into the room. "Some good reason!" she cried. "You dropped this bag full of toys when you tried to get away! Imagine! Taking things from *children!*"

"But I wasn't taking them, dear madam. I was *bringing* them! Ho ho ho."

"You can ho ho ho all you want, but you won't fool us!" insisted Grandpa Forgetful. "We know perfectly well that *Santa Claus* is the only one who ever climbs down chimneys bringing gifts! And he never arrives on the Fourth of July!"

"That's very true," sighed the man in the chimney. "It doesn't *snow* on the Fourth of July, either."

The Forgetfuls all turned to the window. "So that's what that stuff is!" cried Mrs. Forgetful. "I couldn't imagine why it was so *dusty* outside!"

FORGETFUL
BEARS

"Merry Christmas, one and all! And now, would you get me down, please?"

The Forgetfuls tugged and pulled until Santa was free.

"Thank you very much," said Santa. "Here are some gifts for Phoebe and Roger. I must be on my way now."

"But just look at your clothes," exclaimed Mrs. Forgetful. "They're filthy! You don't set *one* foot out of this house until you're as neat and clean as when you climbed into our chimney!"

So Santa Claus took Mr. Forgetful's robe and gave him his red suit. "I'm really in a big hurry. Will you promise to do these quickly?"

"Absolutely!" Racing down to the basement, Mr. Forgetful popped Santa's things into the machine. Then he waited right there until they were washed and dried.

"I kept my promise!" he told himself proudly. "But who did I make it to?"

Coming up the stairs, he noticed there was someone sitting in the kitchen with Mrs. Forgetful and Grandpa.

"I thought that was *my* robe," said Mr. Forgetful to himself. "But if it belongs to him, then *these* clothes must be mine." So he put them on.

Just then he heard some banging noises coming from the roof.

Mr. Forgetful went up to have a look — and saw a big sleigh filled to the top with presents. In front of it stood eight reindeer, snorting and stomping because they wanted to be on their way.

Mr. Forgetful looked at them, then at his red suit. "Well, I won't keep you waiting a moment longer!" he cried. And jumping into the sleigh, he shouted, "On Grumpy! On Sneezy! On Dopey! On Bashful!"

He couldn't understand why they didn't move.

Suddenly two windows flew open, and two little heads popped out. "Oh, look!" Phoebe cried to her brother. "It's Dad!"

The children threw on their coats and were up on the roof in a flash.

Mr. Forgetful was glad to see them. "Does anybody remember how to start this thing?"

"Sure, Dad!" Roger picked up the reins and shouted,
"On Robin! On Batman! On — "

"No, Roger," cried his sister. "Those are not their names!"

"Then what are they?"

"Winnie the Pooh! And Alice! And Christopher Robin!"
The reindeer rolled their eyes and groaned.

"We'll just have to go on foot," said Mr. Forgetful. They
picked up all the presents they could carry. And off they went.

As they walked along, Roger pointed to a house. "Dad, a kid I know lives in there. He's . . . uh . . . he's. . . . Oh, what's-his-name?"

"Hmm. I see an O'Reilly on the mailbox. But no O'Whatshisname."

"Phoebe, you know who I mean! He's the biggest, scariest kid in the whole school."

"Oh, sure! And stuck-up, too. He thinks he's a living doll."

Mr. Forgetful's eyes opened wide. "He's a doll? Then I guess this must be for him." He carried a dollhouse in through one of the windows.

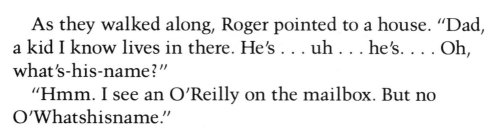

Soon they were all rushing in and out of houses. "Let's see! The red box goes to the boy in the blue house. No, the blue box goes to the girl in the red house! No! That's not it!"

After a while, they were out of gifts. "But there's a boy in that new house!" cried Phoebe. "I can see him sleeping with the light on."

"Let's go home and bring him some of our toys!" suggested Roger. "But we'll leave him a note first that Santa will be back."

"I'll do it," said Phoebe. When she went into the house, the television was on. In the movie that was playing, a lot of cowboys were chasing a lot of Indians. "Oh," she thought, "it's *The Wizard of Oz*! I never remember if Dorothy goes back to Kansas." And she sat down to watch.

When she didn't come out, Roger opened one of the
windows. "Psssst! Pssst!" he called softly. "Where are you?"
"Right here!" said the little boy, jumping up in bed.
"I'm Timmy. Who are you?"

Meanwhile, back at the Forgetfuls' house, Santa Claus was waiting and waiting in the kitchen. It was already morning!

"Why is it taking so long to clean my clothes?"

Mrs. Forgetful went to find out and saw that Santa's suit was gone. So were the toys — and her husband and children.

"Christmas is ruined! Ruined!" cried Santa.

"No, it isn't!" shouted Grandpa, hurrying out of the house. "We'll find them, or my name isn't . . . or my name isn't. . . ?" He jumped into the car and started to drive away.

"Come back! You forgot *us!*" Santa and Mrs. Forgetful yelled until Grandpa came back.

The car whizzed through town. "Stop!" said Santa. "That's one of the places I go to."

He ran to the door and knocked very hard.

A huge bull answered it. *"WELL?"*

"Uh, excuse me. I know that I'm not exactly dressed like Santa Claus, but that's who I am."

"If you've come to take back that dollhouse you left by mistake for my son," he roared, *"FORGET IT!"*

"You mean he already broke it?"

"Of course not! My boy loves that dollhouse! And he's going to keep it!"

"Well, Merry Christmas," said Santa. He walked away thinking, "I wonder who got the football uniform I was going to leave there?"

"Santa! Catch!" Suddenly a football whizzed through an open door across the way, and out burst a football player.

"Is that you, Jennifer, under all that?"

"Yes!" cried the girl, throwing her arms around him. "How did you think of it, Santa? This is so much better than the dollhouse I asked for!"

"I'm so confused," said Santa as he drove off again with Grandpa and Mrs. Forgetful.

Just then, they heard music and singing coming from the house on the corner. Mrs. Forgetful looked in the window. She saw her family inside, dancing.

"In there!" she pointed. Grandpa stopped the car. Then the three of them burst into the house.

Santa was pretty upset with Mr. Forgetful. "Can I *please* have my suit back!"

"Is it yours?" said Mr. Forgetful. "Well, I do beg your pardon. But you really shouldn't go leaving these things around, you know."

"Oh, Santa!" cried Timmy. "Thank you for giving me the best Christmas present ever!"

He took Phoebe and Roger by the hand. "My two new friends!"

Then Timmy's mother made a big Christmas breakfast. And they all sang and laughed and had a wonderful time — which they never forgot!